To Chelsea
— M.M.

On World Series day Matthew was playing a baseball game in his front yard. There was no one there to join his team, so he threw the ball at the wall instead.

"Last of the ninth, it's tied at three. Matthew's up, let's see what he'll do. Wham! He hits it, it could be a homer..."

"Matthew, don't be a turkey!" his mother called out. "Stop bouncing the ball on the house. You're driving me crazy!"

"Matthew breaks for home! Here comes the throw! The catcher's tag! He drops the ball!" Matthew yelled as he slid across the lawn.

He was about to start a victory dance when the neighbor's dog darted in and snatched the ball. Matthew gave chase, but he never had a chance.

"Don't worry," his mother said, when he came in for supper. "He'll soon get tired and bring your ball back. Next time it happens, don't chase him, dear. Tell him to drop it, he probably will."

At bedtime Matthew wasn't tired. He put his radio under his pillow and turned it on low to help him feel sleepy. The baseball game was underway.

"He hits the ball deep in the hole at short..."

"Matthew?"

His mother was coming into his room so Matthew turned off the radio.

"Is that the baseball game I hear?" she asked.

Matthew couldn't say, but when she discovered the radio under his pillow, he was pretty sure it was.

"Go to sleep," she said. "There's lots of time for baseball tomorrow."

She tucked him in and kissed him goodnight. Matthew closed his eyes. As he fell asleep, he wondered what was happening in the big game.

Around about midnight, a baseball flew in through Matthew's window and woke him up. He picked up the ball and ran outside. The midnight turkeys were playing a baseball game on his lawn. The batter was chasing the first base turkey, who was holding the bag out of reach overhead. Matthew ran over and made the tag. "Yer out!" he cried.

"No fair!" the batter yelled. "This guy stole first. Tag him out too!"

Matthew obliged, and when he was through, the rest of the turkeys lined up so he could tag them out as well. "This is the best game I've ever had," Matthew said.

"This is just practice," the turkeys told him. "The real game starts later on. Join our team and you can play too."

A few moments later the team bus arrived. A wrinkled old bird came down the steps.

"This is Buz, our manager," the turkeys explained.

"I want to play on the team," Matthew told him.

"You sure you're a turkey?" the old buzzard asked.

"My mother says I am, sometimes."

"If your mother says so, then I guess it's true," Buz replied. "Still, you never know what an ump might decide. Better put on a disguise."

The turkeys agreed. They gave Matthew feathers to stick in his hat, a yo-yo, some gum, a couple of stickers to wear on his bum, and other such things that a turkey enjoys.

"Turkeyball is easy to play," the turkeys assured him. "All you gotta do is just be yourself and do what you gotta do."

TURKEY TAXI
TR KY

TUR
0

When they got to the Dome, Buz gave his team some advice. "Don't eat hot dogs when you're up at bat, eat 'em on deck or on base," he said. "No sitting in the stands, no eating your hat. No spitting in your shoes, use the ball for that. No dancing in the dugout, no yo-yos in the pen, and absolutely no bungee jumping with less than two outs."

"Ladies and gentlemen, your Toronto Turkeys!" the announcer announced.

The crowd went crazy; the turkeys did too. They kicked off their shoes and raced out of the dugout, gobbling and giggling and wiggling their bums as they slid into all the bases.

"Looks like the boys mean business tonight," Buz said with a grin.

The Toronto Turkeys were playing the Montreal Posties, but the way they played was a little bit strange. Halfway through the top of the first, the third base turkey threw a barbecue on the pitcher's mound. His teammates dropped in from time to time, so Matthew had lots of places to play. First he tried second, second he tried first. Then he played left and right simultaneously, which is quite hard to do if you're eating too.

The game took a while. The Posties' pitcher had a slow delivery, and the catcher had his dog along to return the ball to the mound. At the end of three, it was twenty to ten. At the end of four it was half past thirty. No one was sure what it was after five.

By the top of the sixth, when they added the score it was more or less sixty to fifty-four, bases loaded, nobody out. Matthew was playing in the hole at short. Crack! The batter took a tremendous whack. The ball went straight up in the air.

"I got it, I got it," the turkeys all yelled. They threw off their hats and their uniforms too, and danced around in their underwear underneath where the ball might come down.

It was Matthew who finally made the catch. He scrambled out of the hole at short and tagged all the Posties runners.

"Yer out! Yer out! And so are you! The batter's out too!" the umpire shouted. "An unassisted quadruple play!"

"Actually, we only need three of the outs right now," Matthew told him.

"Fine by me," the ump replied. "Save the fourth till later."

The Posties' manager came out of the dugout and started arguing. He bumped the ump and made a big scene. The Montreal Posties got into the act. They threw lots of mail up into the air and sat on packages. The turkeys liked to argue too, so they bumped each other until they fell down. Everyone had a very good time, so when the umps tried to throw them all out, they threw out the umps instead.

KEYS
KEYS

When it was time for the seventh inning stretch, the Toronto Turkeys jumped up on the dugout and sang along with their loyal fans.

Okay! Turkeys! Let's eat food!
We got hot dogs, and some cola,
We got pretzels, and slushies, and ice cream too,
We got some popcorn and some peanuts,
We got natchos with lots of cheesy goo.
What d'ya want? Let's eat food!
Okay! Turkeys! Let's eat food!
Okay! Turkeys! Let's eat food!

When the Toronto Turkeys came up to bat in the bottom of the ninth, the score was tied at seventy-four. The Posties' pitcher had a sore arm, so he staged a walkout and left the field. The rest of the infield joined the strike, and sat on the ground all around the mound. Their manager called the pen.

"Bring in The Supervisor," he ordered.

The Supervisor took the mound. He wore a tie and his shirt was clean, but his face wasn't shaved and his eyes were mean. He struck out the first two turkeys he faced with fastballs. Then it was Matthew's turn. The Supervisor glared at him with a murderous frown on his face.

"I hope my mom has insurance on me," Matthew told himself nervously.

STRIKE

The first two pitches came in so fast that Matthew never saw them at all. It was 0-and-2, so he closed his eyes. Crack! The ball hit the bat and went straight back. It smacked the Supervisor on his hard hat, and bounced deep in the hole at short.

All the infielders gathered around, but they were still on strike, so no one could jump in to get the ball. Matthew went into his home run trot. He was just about as far as third when he heard the catcher shout, "Go get it boy!"

The catcher's dog streaked away from the plate and went straight to the hole at short. As he jumped in to retrieve the ball, Matthew made a break for home. There might be a play at the plate after all!

Matthew slid home in a cloud of dust, just as the dog arrived. "Yer out, you turkey!" the catcher cried, as he applied the tag.

"Drop it, boy! Drop it!" Matthew yelled.

The dog obediently dropped the ball and began to wag his tail.

"Yer safe! We win! We're Champeens of the Universe!" the Toronto Turkeys shouted. They lifted Matthew up onto their heads and carried him around the Dome in a frenzied conga line.

When the celebration was through, the midnight turkeys took Matthew home.

"Thanks, you guys," Matthew called, as he waved goodbye. "Turkeyball is neat!"

"Come out with us any night you can," the turkeys cried. "You're the very best player our team ever had, and you know how to eat a lot too."

As they drove away, they tossed the game-winning ball on the lawn for Matthew to keep as a souvenir.

"I'll get it tomorrow," Matthew told himself, as he climbed into bed. He yawned once or twice, then he closed his eyes. Soon he was fast asleep.

When Matthew woke up, he jumped out of bed and ran down to get the ball. He held it triumphantly over his head and sang the Toronto Turkeys song as he did a one-man conga line across the lawn. A few moments later, his mother was there in her dressing gown.

"Matthew, you turkey, what are you doing? It's six a.m.!"

"I got the ball!" Matthew told her.

"So I see," his mother said. "The dog must have brought it back in the night."

"Not that ball, Mom — *this* one. This is the ball that made the Toronto Turkeys the Champeens of the Universe! And you know what else? You were absolutely right. When I told the dog to drop the ball, that's exactly what he did! That's how we won the game, so we owe it all to you. I think you deserve a souvenir, too."

Matthew took off his baseball cap and placed it on her head. He could tell from the far away look in her eyes that she liked it a lot.

"You earned it, Mom," Matthew said. Then he led a two-person conga line all the way in to breakfast.